ISBN 0 333 36873 8

First published in 1984 by Macmillan Children's Books a division of Macmillan Publishers Limited, 4 Little Essex Street, London WC2R 3LF and Basingstoke

Associated companies throughout the world.

Printed in Hong Kong

Designed by Sue Williams

British Library Cataloguing in Publication Data

Verschoyle, Teresa
    Hansel and Gretel. – (Favourite fairy stories)
I. Title
823′ 914 [J]   PZ8
ISBN 0-333-36873-8

Hansel and Gretel

retold by by Teresa Verschoyle
illustrated by Ivan Ripley

MACMILLAN

Once a poor woodcutter lived with his son Hansel
and his daughter Gretel in a little hut in a wood.
The children's mother was dead,
and their father had married a new wife.
They were very poor and very hungry.

One night when Hansel and Gretel
were too hungry to sleep,
they heard their stepmother scolding their father.
"There is not a drop of milk in the house,
and hardly a crumb of bread to eat," she grumbled.
"How can we feed two greedy children,
when we have not enough food for ourselves?
In the morning we must leave Hansel and Gretel
so far away in the forest that they will never
find their way home."
"How can I leave my children all alone in the forest
with the wild beasts?" cried the kind woodcutter,
but his wife nagged and scolded until she had her way.

"We can't let her do this," whispered Gretel.
"We must think of a plan."
They talked until they decided what to do.

Much later, when their parents were asleep,
Hansel crept outside into the garden
and filled his pockets with the white pebbles
which shone like silver in the moonlight.
Then he went tiptoe back to bed.

In the morning the stepmother woke up the children
and gave them each a crust of bread.
Then the whole family walked far into the forest
to chop wood, but every now and then
Hansel dropped a white pebble on the path
to mark the way home.
Far away in the middle of the dark forest,
their father built a fire in a glade
and told the children to lie down and rest.
They ate their crusts, and soon fell fast asleep.

When they awoke it was dark and cold.
The fire had gone out,
and their parents were nowhere to be seen.
It was dreadfully lonely.
But when the moon came out,
it made the white pebbles shine like silver.
Hansel and Gretel followed them all the way home.

How glad their father was to see them safe and sound,
but their stepmother had never looked so cross!
Not many nights later the children heard her
nagging her husband again.
"The children must be sent away," she scolded.
"This time we shall leave them even deeper
in the forest, and they will not come back."

Hansel got out of bed again,
but this time the wife had locked the door.
He could not go outside to pick up the white pebbles,
so the two children made a different plan.

Early next day the stepmother gave each of the children
an even smaller crust of bread,
and as they all walked deep into the forest
Hansel dropped a line of breadcrumbs
to mark the way home.
Then the wife sat the children down by a big fire,
and after Gretel had shared her bread with Hansel
they soon fell fast asleep.

When dark night had come,
they awoke and found they were alone.

"Never mind, Hansel," said Gretel to cheer him up.
"Wait till the moon shines on the crumbs."
But the birds of the air had pecked up all the crumbs,
and there were none left to show the way home.
The children wandered all night and all day,
but still they were lost.
They were hungrier than ever
and worn out with walking,
so they lay down together to sleep.

Next morning they wandered sadly deeper and deeper
into the dark ugly forest.
There on a bough sat a beautiful snow-white bird,
singing with all its heart!
The children clapped their hands and ran after the bird
as it flew from tree to tree. It soon led them
to a dear little cottage, all made of gingerbread,
plum cake and sugar.

"Now we can eat as much as we want," Hansel rejoiced as he broke off a piece of the gingerbread roof and crammed it in his mouth, while hungry Gretel took a big bite of sugar door-knob.

Then a voice called from inside,
"Tip-tap, tip-tap, who is tapping at my door?"
"Only the wind," called back the children,
and went on with their feast.
Just then the door flew open,
and out hobbled a bent old woman.
Hansel and Gretel were so frightened
that they dropped their cake,
but the old woman smiled kindly.
"Come along in, dear children," she said.
"You must be hungry after your wanderings,"
and she led them into her snug kitchen.

A good meal of milk and hot pancakes
was spread for them on the table,
and the more the children ate
the more the old woman smiled,
so that she seemed the kindest old woman in the world.
When the children had eaten all they wanted,
she even tucked them in two warm little beds to sleep.

Hansel and Gretel were happy as could be
now they were warm and well fed again,
but they did not know that the old woman
was really a wicked witch, who liked to eat children.
Her red eyes were so bad that she could
hardly see at all, but she had smelt the children
from far away. She had sent the beautiful white bird
and made the gingerbread house
just to trick Hansel and Gretel into coming close
so that she could catch them for dinner.

Next morning she looked to see if the children were
nice and fat. They were too thin to eat yet,
so she pulled Hansel out of bed
and pushed him into a cage in the yard.
"Let me out," called Hansel,
and he beat on the door with his fists,
but it was no use.

Then the witch woke Gretel.
"Get up," she snapped. "Help me cook
something good to fatten up your brother,
and when he is nice and plump I can eat him up."
Gretel had to do as the horrid witch told her.
She washed and scrubbed and cooked all day,
but still went hungry herself.

Every morning the witch went to the cage and said,
"Hansel, stick your little finger through the bars
so that I may feel how plump you are."
But Hansel held out a hard chicken bone
instead of his finger, and the old witch
was tricked and thought he was still too thin.
She could not understand it at all.
"Boys never used to be so skinny," she grumbled.

When a whole month had gone by
and Hansel was still as thin
as ever, the greedy witch
could wait no longer.
"Gretel," she called,
"Fat or thin, I shall
eat Hansel today.
But first we must bake.
Come along now, get
in the oven at once and
see if it is hot enough
for the bread."
But Gretel was not going
to get in the oven and
let the witch
bake her as well as Hansel!
"How do I get in?" she asked.
"I do not know how."

This put the nasty witch in a real rage.
"Like this, you stupid," she said,
and she bent down to look in the oven.
Quickly Gretel pushed her right inside
and slammed the door shut.
How the witch howled,
but Gretel ran away
and let her burn to ashes.

Gretel ran to Hansel in the yard.
She soon unlocked the cage,
and told him the witch was dead.
Hansel jumped out of his cage,
as good as new and a great deal fatter,
and they both danced for joy.

There was nothing to be afraid of any more,
so they went back into the witch's house
to look around. Lo and behold,
there under her bed were boxes of treasure,
full of pearls and gold and diamonds!

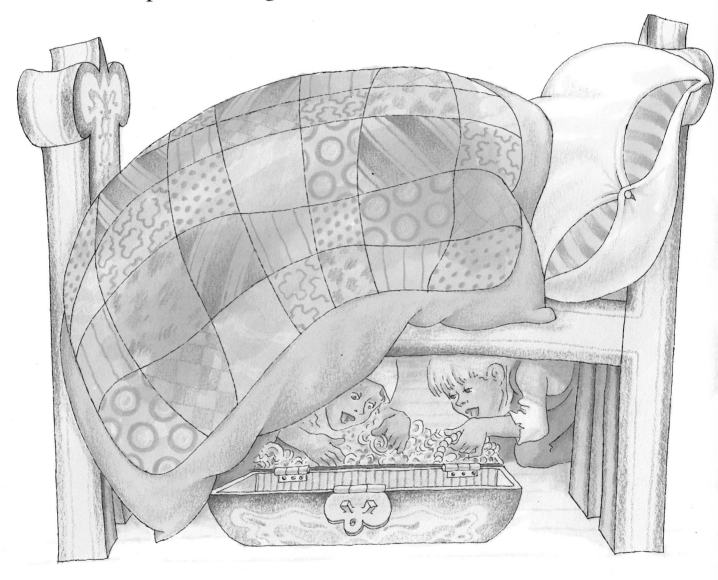

"We shall always have plenty of money
to buy food now," said Hansel
as he filled his pockets with gold coins,
while happy Gretel crammed her apron with jewels.

When they had taken all they could carry
they left the gingerbread house
and set off through the forest.
"We shall find the way home now the witch
and her spells are gone," said Gretel,
but by and by they came to a broad lake
with a white duck swimming on it.
The children could not swim,
but when Gretel called out to the duck,

Little duck with back so white,
Help us cross the lake tonight,

it kindly carried first Hansel
and then Gretel safely across the water.
Gretel kissed the duck and gave her
a necklace of pearls.

When they had gone a little way
they found the path to their own home.

In they ran to find their father
and tell him about the witch and show him
their treasure of pearls and gold and diamonds.
The poor woodcutter had not had one happy moment
since he left the children in the forest,
and he was overjoyed to see them.
His wife was dead now,
and the three of them lived happily ever after
in their little hut in the wood.